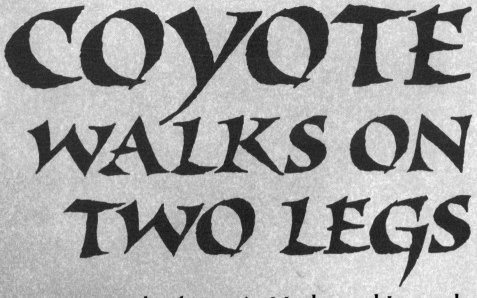

COYOTE WALKS ON TWO LEGS

A Book of Navajo Myths and Legends

collected and retold by
GERALD HAUSMAN

Illustrated by
FLOYD COOPER

Philomel Books   New York

AUTHOR'S NOTE

The stories in this book were originally told to me by my Navajo friend, Bluejay, or as I have always called him, Jay. He learned these sacred creation legends from his father, who was a medicine man. It is necessary, in the Navajo way, to wait for the proper time to tell a tale. Therefore, many years passed between stories; perhaps more than thirty altogether.

"Coyote's New Coat" and "The Day Magpie Tricked Coyote" are what we might call "double trickster" tales. For they show how a master gamester like Coyote can be completely fooled by his own desire.

We generally think of Coyote as a harmless, good-natured goof, but as "The Great Flood" explains, Coyote's interference can also do harm. I remember asking Jay if he thought Coyote—in this particular tale—was "a bad guy." He answered, "Coyote brings change; sometimes good, sometimes bad. But always his mischief causes us to experience new ways of doing things, new ways of knowing. This is his great gift to The People."

In "The Guardian of the Corn," we discover that corn is a sacred food that must be watched with care. Jay explained that First Man and First Woman are always drawn as if they came out of the earth like the corn. "The People," he told me, "and the corn are as one."

It is good, then, to remember that Coyote, in these myths, walks on two legs and shares the same world that we do. We are not strangers and the Navajos say that we once spoke the same language. We should also realize that while Coyote's bravery is often foolery, his love of leaping into the unknown is what encourages us to be alive. Long live Coyote the foolish, Coyote the brave.

Gerald Hausman
Tesuque, New Mexico

For Marie
— G.H.

For Patti
— F.C.

The Great Flood

In the beginning there was no sun, moon or stars.

But in the East
There was the thing named White Dawn,
Which appeared each morning.

And in the South
There was the thing named Blue Dawn,
Which appeared each day at midday.

And in the West
There was the thing called Yellow Dawn,
Which appeared each day at the close of day.

This was the world that the Animal People knew.

Among them lived one who was brave and foolish.
He was named First Angry, but that is another story.
We will call him Coyote.

Coyote was sent to discover the Dawns
But instead he found two water-monster babies
Who lived with their parents
In two large springs that came out of the earth.

Now Coyote was a natural born trickster and thief
And he stole the water-monster babies,
And after this the Great Flood began.

The water at the head of the two springs
Rose so fast the Animal People had to run to high
Ground to get away from it.

And still, it kept rising, higher and higher.

At last the water rose so high upon the earth
The Animal People
Gathered bags of corn and seeds
And climbed to the top of White Mountain.
But it was not long before White Mountain
Was covered with water.
Then they climbed Blue Mountain
Until it was covered, Yellow Mountain
Until it was covered, and lastly,
Black Mountain.

The water rose to the top of Black Mountain
And the Animal People
Planted a hollow reed
In the earth before the water
Could cover it.

Into the reed all the Animal People went.
The last one into the reed was Turkey,
Whose tail-feathers were whitened
In the foamy water.

Turkey's tail-feathers, as we all know,
Have remained white all this time…
But that is another story.
What happened when the Animal People
Got to the top of the reed
Is what this story is about.

When they could go no further
For there was nowhere to go —
Locust opened his bow of darkness
And shot a sacred arrow into the sky.

The arrow of Locust made a hole
In the sky and through the hole
The Animal People passed
Into the next world.

And that was how the Great Flood ended
And the new world began.

First Angry

In the beginning of the new world
The Two-Legged People lived among
The Animal People,
And they were happy living together.

It was First Man
Who ordered Gopher to go under the ground
Because Gopher was the one who brought
Toothache into the world.

First Man knew what was best
For the Animal People.
So he told the birds to live in the sky,
And he told the lizards to live in the rocks
And the snakes to live there also.

He told the beavers and otters
To live in the water,
And all was well,
Until Coyote showed his face.

As everyone knows, Coyote caused
The Great Flood.
First Man knew he could not stop
Coyote from going anywhere he pleased,

But he did have the power to give him
A name Coyote would not like.

The name he gave to him was
He Who Minds Everybody's Business.

When Coyote heard this name, he got mad.
He would not stop yelling about it.
So First Man said he would give him
Another name, but this name would be
The last one and he would have to take it
Or leave it.

Coyote said he would take it.

The name First Man gave him was
He Who Gets Angry First.

Coyote liked the name very much.
But he soon shortened it to
First Angry
Which is what we call him today.

The Day Magpie Tricked Coyote

One day Coyote
Sat under a juniper tree
And watched Magpie
Play the game Throw Away Eyes.

Magpie flew into the air
Threw his head up, down, and off to the side
And suddenly both of his eyes
Jumped out of his eye-sockets.

But before his eyes fell to the ground,
Magpie dived down,
Caught them in his beak,
And put them back in his head.

It was a great trick
And Coyote wanted to try it.

"I do not think you can do that trick,"
Magpie said.

"Why?" Coyote asked.

"I think only Magpies can do this trick,"
Magpie said.

"If you teach me Throw Away Eyes,
I will sing the Magpie Song," Coyote said.

Now Magpie liked nothing so well
As this song which was all about him.
Coyote started singing the song.
Magpie listened until the song was done.

Magpie was pleased from his crown-feathers
To his claws,
And he showed Coyote
How to throw away his eyes
And catch them up
Before they fell to the ground.

Coyote was so eager to throw his eyes away
That he threw himself up, down,
And off to the side
And his eyes went out of his head.

They went up into the air
And fell on the sand
And rolled away.
Coyote could not see:
He was blind as Cousin Bat.

"Eyes, come back—" Coyote howled,
But his eyes kept rolling,
And some People say they never stopped.

Magpie said, "You were supposed
To catch them up the way I did."

Coyote was not listening.
He was thinking that he would never see
The light of day again.
He wanted to cry, but without his eyes
The tears would not come.

Magpie did not want to sit around all day
Watching Coyote drag his tail
In the sand.
He wanted to tell his friends
How he tricked the trickster,
How he played Coyote for a fool.

Just then Bluejay came by.

Bluejay was a noisy person
But he could also be helpful.
When he saw Coyote walking
With his head hanging down,
He asked what was wrong.

"I played the game they call
Throw Away Eyes," Coyote said.

"Never mind," Bluejay said.
"I know how to find you another pair of eyes — "

Then Bluejay rolled
Two bright beads of pine-sap into a pair
Of eyes for Coyote.

The moment Bluejay put the new eyes
In Coyote's head, Coyote could see again.

He danced around in a circle
Shouting: "Magpie, my eyes are back —
Now I will get even!"

He was so excited
That he forgot to thank
Bluejay for helping him.
He danced up, down, and all around —
But he did not dance off to the side.
And his new eyes stayed in his head.

But it was a very hot day
And as Coyote danced around
He kept looking at the sun,
And pretty soon
His eyes started to melt.

The moment he felt his eyes melting,
Coyote ran away from the sun
And chased his shadow.
After a time, his eyes cooled off
But now there were two soot-streaks
On either side of his face.
He tried to rub them off
But the soot-streaks stayed.

Some People say those soot-streaks
Remind Coyote of the day that Magpie
Tricked him.
They say he learned his lesson
And now he takes care of his yellow
Pine-sap eyes.
But there are those who say
That if the same thing happened to Coyote
Today, this very day,
He would lose his eyes in the same old way.

Coyote's New Coat

Coyote was out walking one day
When he saw Mother Deer
And two spotted fawns.

"You are looking lovely today,"
Coyote said to Mother Deer.
"But your children are even
More lovely than you —
Tell me, how did they
Get those pretty white spots?"

"That is easy to say,"
Said Mother Deer.
"First you make a big fire
Of cedar sticks.
Then you wait for Wind to come
Up to play.
Wind blows the sparks,

And that is what makes those
Pretty spots."

"Is that all there is to it?"
Asked Coyote.

"That is all," said Mother Deer,
And she took her young ones
And went on her way.

Coyote thought to himself:
"How fine I would look
In a fancy spotted coat!"

And he built a cedar fire
So that when Wind came up
To play
The sparks went like moths
Into Coyote's coat
And made holes
All the way to his skin.

The other Animal People laughed
Out loud when they saw how silly
Coyote looked,
But Mother Deer
Only smiled and said:
"Now every year Coyote
Will grow a new coat of fur."

And it is true: every year
Just before winter
Coyote sheds his old ragged
Coat and gets a new glossy one.

Today he knows that he cannot
Ever look like a little fawn.
He can only look like himself,
Coyote.

The Guardian of the Corn

One day Coyote was hungry
And he asked Horned Toad,
The Guardian of the Corn,
To give him some of her
Best ears.

"You should grow your own corn,"
Horned Toad said.

"That takes too long," Coyote said.
"Besides, I am hungry for some corn right now."

But Horned Toad
Did not want to give
Her corn to such a lazy
Person.

"Go away," she said
And she pointed
The horns on top of her head
At Coyote.

Coyote pretended to sniff
At the Wind,
Then he snatched up
The Guardian of the Corn
And swallowed her whole.

Now there was no one
Around to scold him
And Coyote, being
Very hungry, went
Into Horned Toad's
Cornfield and ate
As much as he wanted.

He was so stuffed
He could not move.
He lay in the sun
With his paws over
His eyes and went
To sleep.

Just then
Raven flew overhead.

"Can I have some of your corn?" Raven asked.

"You should grow your own corn," Coyote said.

"That takes too long," Raven said.
"Besides I am hungry for some corn right now."

Then, as Coyote
Was about to say "Go away,"
He felt something sharp
Stick him in the stomach.

"What is that?" he said.

"What is what?" Raven asked, circling overhead.

"I will teach him what that is —" said a tiny voice.

It was Horned Toad
Talking from down inside
Coyote's belly.
Then she poked him four times
With her two-horned head,
And Coyote let out a loud burp.

"What was that you said?" Raven asked.

Coyote tried to talk,
But Horned Toad poked
Him four more times
In the belly
And he started spitting
Corn kernels everywhere.

"You do not have to be impolite," Raven said.
"I know when I am not wanted."
And he went off.

Presently Coyote felt very sick.
He was still spitting corn kernels
When Horned Toad
Flew out of his mouth.

"Let that be a lesson to you," she said.
But Coyote was so sick
He did not hear a word.

Today, if you should come
To Navajoland, you would see
That Horned Toad is still
The Guardian of the Corn
And that Coyote is still
The trickster he always was.